Pea Soup Fog

By Connie Macdonald Smith

Illustrations by Jen Cart

Down East Books / Camden, Maine

Printed in China by Oceanic Graphic Printing

2   4   5   3   1

ISBN: 0-89272-643-1

Down East Books
Camden, Maine
A division of Down East Enterprise,
publishers of *Down East* magazine

Book Orders: 800-766-1670
www.downeastbooks.com

Library of Congress Control Number: 2004109061

Dedication

Connie: To my father, Dr. Roderick A. Macdonald, who told me once, "You are smart enough to write a book."

Jen: To all the people who modeled for the pictures in this book: Sarah and Julie, Chris and Juliet, Kate and Zack.

Fog settled like twilight upon the small village by the sea.

Wind chilled the fog and the bone-cold villagers shook and stumbled their way about because no one could see anything at all.

"It gets foggy when Grammy makes soup," said a tiny girl with goose bumps. But no one believed her. No one at all.

"This fog is from the butcher smoking his great hams," said one villager. "Can't you smell them?"

"Then the butcher should know how to get rid of the fog," said another.

So the villagers and the tiny girl stumbled their way to the butcher's shop.

"Do you know how to get rid of the fog?" asked the villagers.

"I do," said the butcher, exercising his wits in a cloudy sort of way.

"I will slash the fog to shreds with my butcher knife," he said. "That will get rid of the fog."

So the butcher slashed and sliced the fog to ribbons.

But the fog did not go away. No way. Not at all.

The butcher blushed like a crimson beet.

"It gets foggy when Grammy . . ." began the tiny girl.

"This fog is not from my shop," interrupted the butcher.

"It is from the baker baking loaves in her cavernous ovens. Can't you catch the smell of them?"

"Ahhh," said the villagers, "we can smell the bread."

"Then the baker should know how to get rid of the fog," said the butcher.

"Please, may I have a bone before we go," asked the tiny girl, "since you have a pile of them?"

"Of course," said the butcher, "since I have a pile of them."

The villagers sighed and shivered and shuffled their feet.

And the fog got thicker and colder while the butcher, the villagers, and the tiny girl stumbled their way to the baker's shop.

"Do you know how to get rid of the fog?" asked the villagers.

"I do," said the baker, frowning in a muddled sort of way. "I will stuff it into my flour sacks. That will get rid of the fog."

So she filled her flour sacks to bursting with fog.

But the fog did not go away. No way. Not at all.

The baker blushed like a scarlet cherry.

"It gets foggy when Grammy . . ." began the tiny girl.

"This fog is not from my shop," interrupted the baker. "It is from the candle-maker melting her wax. Can't you catch the smell of it?"

"Ahhh," said the villagers, "we can smell the wax."

"Then the candle-maker should know how to get rid of the fog," said the baker.

"Please, may I have a loaf of bread before we go," asked the tiny girl, "since you have a heap of them?"

"Of course," said the baker, "since I have a heap of them."

The villagers sighed and shivered and shuffled their feet.

And the fog got thicker and colder while the butcher, the baker, the villagers, and the tiny girl stumbled their way to the candle-maker's shop.

"Do you know how to get rid of the fog?" asked the villagers.

"I do," said the candle-maker, racking her brain in a foggy sort of way. "I will burn it away," she said. "That will get rid of the fog."

So the candle-maker lit all the candles in her shop.

But the fog did not go away. No way. Not at all.

The candle-maker did not blush like a crimson beet, or a scarlet cherry, or even a purple plum. Instead, she threw up her hands and said, "I do not know where this fog is coming from."

"Then what shall we do?" cried the villagers.

"I smell soup," said the tiny girl. "Can't you catch the smell of it?"

"Ahhh, we smell soup, too," said the villagers.

"Grammy's soup will take our chill away," said the girl. "I will take you there."

"Please, may I have a candle before we go," she asked, "since you have a rack of them?"

"Of course," said the candle-maker, "since I have a rack of them." The candle-maker took a candle from her rack, lit the wick, and gave it to the tiny girl.

The villagers sighed and shivered and stomped their feet.

And the fog got thicker and colder while the butcher, the baker, the candle-maker, and the villagers followed their noses and the tiny girl to Grammy's cottage.

The tiny girl knocked. The door creaked open.

"Sakes alive!" said Grammy. "The whole village is at my door."

"We are frozen to the bone," said the tiny girl.

"Come in, then, and warm up," said Grammy, winking at the tiny girl.

"I made pea soup."

"We brought a bone to flavor the soup, bread to share, and a candle to brighten the table," said the tiny girl.

Grammy ladled out the soup from her kettle until it was bone-dry.

"Now we are warm," said the tiny girl after everyone had eaten. "We can go home and think how to get rid of this fog," she said with a wink at Grammy.

The villagers tipped their hats, patted their full, round bellies, and said their goodbyes to Grammy.

When they stepped outside, the fog was all gone and the sun was shining.

Grammy's Split-Pea Soup

1 meaty ham bone

1-lb bag of split peas

8 cups of water

2 medium potatoes, peeled and cubed

2 large onions, chopped

2 medium carrots, cut up

2 cups of cooked ham, cubed

½ cup of celery, chopped

5 tsp. chicken bouillon granules

1 tsp. each of marjoram, poultry seasoning, sage, dried basil

½ tsp pepper

Dash of salt (optional)

Bring all ingredients to a boil and cook 1 to 1½ hours, stirring occasionally, until vegetables and peas are tender. You can wait and add the cubed ham when the peas and vegetables are almost done.